Secrets of the Canyon

Colleen L. Reece

Books by Colleen L. Reece

JumpStart! (Junior Devotional)
Mike
Secrets of the Canyon
Secrets of the Forest

Secrets of the Canyon

Colleen L. Reece

Pacific Press®
Publishing Association

Nampa, Idaho | Oshawa, Ontario, Canada
www.pacificpress.com

Designed by Patricia S. Wegh
Cover and interior illustrations by Mary Bausman

Additional copies of this book can be obtained by calling toll-free
1-800-765-6955 or by visiting http://www.adventistbookcenter.com.

Library of Congress Cataloging-in-Publication data:
Reece, Colleen Loraine, 1935-
    Secrets of the canyon
    1. Natural history—Juvenile works. I. Title

                        508

ISBN 978-0-8280-1389-5

August 2015

Dedication

Many thanks
to my family for all their help
with researching and remembering.

Note to Readers

T hose of you who like *Secrets of the Forest* can now share more adventures with the Reynolds family. New readers will have a great time getting acquainted and discovering many wonders of creation. All we have to do is follow Dad's advice: "Learn to stop, look, and listen."

My brothers and I grew up near Darrington, a small western Washington logging town. Tall trees and mountains surrounded our home, once a one-room school. Mom had taught grades 1-8 (15 students) in what became our kitchen and dining room. My bedroom had been the coatroom.

Our woodsman father and outdoor-loving mother showed us how God created an entire community in the forests, rivers, and fields behind our home.

God's mysteries lurk not only in the forest, or in Darrington. You can discover those wonders wherever you live. *Secrets of the Canyon* shows how a surprise vacation provides a path to new experiences and knowledge. It has a gazillion interesting, often funny or incredible nature facts. The book also helps answer Cari's rhyming question that makes her family laugh:

"What did God do for the kangaroo?

And for the other animals, too?"

If you enjoy reading and hearing my stories half as much as I did living and writing them, you're in for a wonderful time!

Your author friend,
Colleen L. Reece

Contents

The Gray Squirrel

1

Stop, Look, 'n' Lis'n

Five-going-on-6-year-old Cari Reynolds slowly sat down on the top step of her home a few miles from the little logging town of Darrington, Washington. June sunlight warmed her face and bare arms. Cari wiggled her toes. She loved going barefoot, but it had rained almost every day all spring. That meant wearing shoes until "the freeze went out of the ground," as Mom said. The girl was glad summer had finally come. The earth and moss felt good beneath her feet.

The front door of the old-fashioned white house that had once been a one-room school-house flew open. Once upon a time, before Dad and Mom Reynolds got married, Mom had taught all eight grades there. Now Cari's almost 11-year-old brother Andy burst out. He raced across the wide porch and plopped down beside his sister. "Whatcha doing, Cari?" he asked.

"Per-pre-ten-din' to be Dad. Shh." She put her fingers over her mouth.

Andy grinned, thinking of their tall logger father, whose blue eyes and brown hair matched his children's. "You'll have to grow a whole lot to be Dad," he teased. "So how come you're pretending to be him?"

"Don't you r'member what he said?" Cari looked surprised. Raising her small chin, she quoted, " 'If you want to learn secrets of the forest you have to stop, look, 'n' lis'n.' " She pointed a chubby finger toward the base of one of the enormous fir trees that surrounded the house. "Look. There's a banker."

"Right." Andy forgot to be quiet and laughed out loud. The gray squirrel with the white chest dropped the cone it was holding and whisked up the tree. *Brrr-scree. Brrr-scree,* it scolded. Its bushy tail twitched, then curled up behind its back, balancing it on a sturdy limb.

Cari sighed. "You scared him."

"He isn't really scared, just careful," Andy explained. "Sorry. It's just that he looks so much like our Darrington banker I can't help laughing. Mr. Davis always wears a gray suit and a white shirt.

Only he stores away money, not acorns and nuts, like Mr. Squirrel."

Cari began to giggle. "Wouldn't it be funny to have a bank full of acorns and nuts?" She took in a deep breath. "Summer smells so good."

Andy started to tease her some more, but thought better of it. Besides, Cari was right. The sharp tang of fir and pine needles tickled his nose. Brightly blooming flowers in the large hanging baskets on the porch sweetened the air. Even the dust smelled summerish. "I love summertime," he told his little sister. "I like school, but it's fun to have more time to run and play."

"And go with Dad and Mom to see God's forest com-commun—"

"Community," Andy finished for her. He bounded off the porch and found a wide blade of grass. Putting it between his thumbs, he blew hard. It vibrated and made a horrible noise.

Mrs. Reynolds came running. "My goodness! Is there a wild animal in our yard?" she asked, blue eyes twinkling in her pretty face. "Oh! It's not an animal after all. It's an Andy-mal."

Her son groaned at her joke, but Cari clapped her hands and danced down the steps. "A nandy-mal! Andy is a nandy-mal."

Smile wrinkles crinkled around Mom's mouth and eyes. "That's Andy-mal, not nandy-mal, and I made up the word."

"That's funny." Cari giggled some more.

Andy turned a lopsided cartwheel, then lost his balance and landed on the soft, thick mat of needles under the tree where Mr. Squirrel still chattered. "Not as funny as some of the names of real animals."

Cari opened her blue eyes wide. "What are we going to do this summer?" she wanted to know. "You and Dad already showed us the secrets in the forest."

"Yeah," Andy said from his comfortable position on the ground. "Bankers and builders and all that stuff on our posters." He lay so quietly their squirrel friend crept down the tree trunk and perched on a limb closer to the watching boy. "I wish—"

Mom and Cari didn't learn what Andy wished. A distant, but familiar rumble up by Green's Pond warned them a vehicle was coming down the road in front of their country home. ●

2

Crew Bus Is Coming!

The noise grew louder, closer. Andy sprang to his feet and grabbed Cari's hand. "Crew bus is coming!" He ran toward the mailbox that sat back from the road in front of their house. Meeting Dad when he swung down the steps of the old bus was always fun. No matter how tired or dirty he looked from working hard in the woods all day, Dad's wide grin always spread across his face.

Like the sun coming out from behind a cloud, Andy thought. He didn't say it out loud. It didn't sound cool. Not that Dad would care. His keen eyes, so like Andy's, saw a whole lot. They told Andy even more. Dad didn't have to say a single word to show he understood. Andy just knew. It made him feel good inside.

Cari's shorter legs hurried to keep up with her older brother. "Crew bus comin'," she echoed. "Do you think Dad left something in his lunch bucket?" she anxiously added.

"I hope so." Andy grinned. "Mom's a great cook, but it's fun when Dad doesn't eat all his lunch. His leftover half sandwiches and cookies are so good!"

"Me, too." Cari licked her lips and leaned forward to look up the road. The lumbering crew bus had just rounded the corner where the long, straight road curved up and out of sight above Green's Pond. "I see it!" the girl shrieked.

Andy caught her hand in his. "Stay behind the mailbox. You know the rules."

"I am," she told him.

"You looked like you weren't going to be," he mumbled. Dad and Mom depended on him to look out for Cari when they weren't around. Now he kept hold of her hand so she wouldn't run out to meet Dad when he got off the bus.

The brakes on the crew bus screeched and squealed when the vehicle rolled to a stop. The men on the right side waved to Andy and Cari. The children smiled and waved back. The good-natured driver called, "Hello, young 'uns," as he always did. Dad had told the children how much the driver and other workers enjoyed seeing them run out to meet the bus.

"How come Dad is so slow?" Cari demanded, as usual.

Andy squashed his own impatience and told her, also as usual, "He has to get his tools. And his lunch bucket."

Dad stepped down and called over his shoulder, "Good night." He headed for Cari and Andy. A chorus of good nights from the bus followed him.

"They like Dad, don't they?" Cari asked as their father slowly came toward them.

"Yeah." Andy thought of a conversation with Mom from several months earlier. It followed a chance meeting with one of the loggers in the grocery store. The big man had told the Reynoldses what a swell guy Dad was. "None better," he gruffly added. "He stands for what he believes, but doesn't preach at the rest of us. That's what I call a real Christian." Then the logger had turned on his heel and walked away.

"What does he mean?" Cari had whispered.

"It's a great compliment," Mom had explained. "Dad tries to be like Jesus wherever he is."

Cari had had more questions. "How does that man know Dad's a Christian if he doesn't preach?"

"Darrington is a small town. Word gets around. People know we go to church. They also know Dad is fair and honest. He does more than his share of hard jobs. And he's also always there for anyone in trouble. What people *are* counts a whole lot more than what they *say*."

Cari still wasn't satisfied. "Doesn't Dad *ever* say at work he loves God?"

Mom had looked surprised. "Of course. When we try to be like Jesus, it makes people curious. They want to know what makes us different. Dad and I also make sure to give God the credit for things like making me well when I was so sick."

"I want to be like Dad—and you—when I grow up," Cari announced.

Me, too. But Andy had only said it in his heart.

"Thanks, but it's better to try to be like Jesus," Mom had quietly told them. "Dad and I make mistakes. God forgives us, of course, but we're not perfect." She smiled. "It's fine to love and appreciate Dad and me, but always remember: the real hero is Jesus."

"Maybe so," Andy now muttered to himself as Dad hugged Cari, handed her his lunch bucket, then turned to his son. "But Dad and Mom's gotta be 'way ahead of whoever's in second place!" he told himself. ●

God paints the sky.

Secret in
the Yard

Dad laughed and talked so much during supper it made Andy suspicious. He swallowed a mouthful of mashed potatoes and gravy, then asked, "Something funny's going on around here. You're usually so tired you don't talk a lot until after supper, Dad. What's happening?"

"Hap'ning," his sister echoed.

Dad tried to look innocent and failed miserably. "I'll tell you after supper," he promised.

"Do you know?" Andy asked Mom.

She shook her head. "Whatever your father's up to is as much a mystery to me as to you." She forked a piece of tossed salad, her eyes sparkling like two mountain lakes. "It must be nice, though. Dad's been grinning ever since he washed up and we came to the table."

Cari wiggled in her chair. "Hurry and eat fast, Andy, so we can hear the s'prise."

"How do you know it's a surprise, young lady?" Dad asked.

"Easy." Cari laughed. "I don't know what it is. Mom doesn't know. Even Andy doesn't know. So it has to be a s'prise." She took a bite of applesauce. The cinnamon on top left a ring around her mouth. "Did God make more secrets today so we could learn about them?" she asked.

Andy hid his face in his napkin to keep from laughing and hurting his sister's feelings. He saw the corners of Mom's mouth twitch. Cari came up with the most unusual questions! Sometimes the family forgot she was still not quite 6 years old.

"I don't know what secrets God may have made today, Cari," he told his daughter. "I do know if Mom agrees, we're going to see and learn about a whole lot more secrets God created. Some are *verrry* old and mysterious." His eyes twinkled, and he looked pleased with himself.

"Goody!" Cari clapped her hands. "I love, love, love secr'ts."

"So do I." Andy felt his heart thump with excitement. Dad had learned many wonderful and curious things while working in the woods. He never seemed to run out of stories about the world

God had created. "Where are they?" Andy burst out. "The new secrets?"

"Some are far away." Dad chuckled until laugh lines creased his face. "Others are as near as our own backyard."

"Far and near. Far and near. Secrets, secrets, far and near," Cari sang.

"Finish your applesauce," Mom told her. She looked at Dad. "No more talk about secrets until supper's over. OK?"

He glanced out the large, many-paned window of the dining room. More sunshine had replaced a brief, unexpected summer shower. "We may not be able to wait that long. If we go outside now, we'll be able to see one of God's most beautiful secrets. It won't hang around long enough for us to finish eating." He put down his napkin and looked at Mom.

"Please, may we go see?" Andy pleaded.

"Of course." Mom smiled at her family. "Lead on, Mr. Nature Guide," she told Dad. "I hope your secret is what I think it is."

"Thanks, Mom." "Thanks." The children scrambled off their chairs and ran after their father. They crossed the kitchen and wide enclosed back porch. Dad led them past the birdhouse on a tall pole and the post with its basketball hoop. Mom and the children followed his long-legged strides to the open area by the birch tree. There Dad pointed to the sky. "Look."

Everyone glanced up. A gorgeous rainbow spread from the top of one mountain across the sky to the top of another. Rosy light spilled on upturned faces and made them look pink. Cari jumped up and down and exclaimed, "God painted the sky!"

"He did more than that," Mom said. "Remember the story of Noah and the ark? And what happened after the rain stopped and the floodwaters went down?"

"I do," Andy quickly answered. "God promised Noah and his family He would never again destroy the earth with a flood. Then God put a rainbow in the clouds as a sign to help people always remember His promise."

"It is called the everlasting covenant," Dad said. Cari looked puzzled and he explained, "Everlasting means forever, without end. Covenant is a binding agreement between two or more persons; in this case, God and His people."

"Cool." Andy stared at the sky. It was exciting to know God loved the world and His people so much. Even before Jesus came, God had made a promise that would last forever! ●

4

Buried Treasure

ari's face showed she cared more about the rainbow than big words. "Mom, is there really a pot of gold at the end of the rainbow?"

"Why don't we go see?" Andy teased. "One end of the rainbow has moved to our yard. We'll find out if there's treasure buried beneath it." He hurried toward the spot where the dancing colors shimmered just above the ground.

Cari ran after him. When she got there, she cried out, "Where did it go? Oh, over there!" She pointed a chubby finger and raced to a different place. The same thing happened again and again. At last Cari said in a disappointed voice, "How can we find a pot of gold when the end of the rainbow keeps moving? Besides, it's going away." She sighed.

Cari was right. The rainbow slowly faded and disappeared.

"The gold at the end of the rainbow is just a legend, which means a story someone made up," Mom said. "However, there really *is* a pot of gold in our yard. I put it there myself. Yesterday."

"Where, Mom? Give us a hint," they teased.

Her laugh made the corners of the children's mouths turn up in a smile. "I buried part of it in the ground. The rest is in plain sight."

Around and around the large yard Cari and Andy raced, looking for a place where they might find buried treasure. When they were out of breath, Andy suggested, "Let's stop and think. What did Mom do yesterday? It must have been when I was at the neighbors."

"I know! I know!" Cari ducked past him and hurried to a rock garden that circled the base of an enormous fir tree. "Mom planted flowers. Look! Some are white and some are yellow."

Andy grunted. "I should have thought of it sooner. Those yellow flowers are called pot of gold. Mom buried the roots so they would grow."

Cari ran to their parents and gave each a big hug. "We found the buried treasure," she said. "We have our really truly, very own, pot of gold, even though we couldn't catch the rainbow."

Andy loped over to his family. "Yeah. Now

let's go finish supper." He grinned at Dad. "The sooner we get through, the sooner we'll find out what Dad's up to."

"Are you absolutely, positively sure I'm up to something?"

"Better than that. Absotively, posilutely," Andy told him.

"'Tively, 'lutely," Cari echoed and ran toward the back door as fast as she could go.

"We'll clear the table, but leave the dishes until we hear Dad's surprise," Mom decided. She looked as eager as Andy felt—if such a thing were possible! He felt he'd burst if Dad didn't hurry and tell them his surprise.

A few minutes later Dad looked around the circle of faces. Andy sprawled on the rug in front of the sofa, one of his favorite places to relax. Cari sat on Mom's lap. Dad leaned back in his big swing rocker chair. "Ready?" he asked.

"Ready," the others said together.

"I won't even ask you to guess, because you couldn't. Not if you lived to be older than Methuselah."

"My goodness," Mom gasped. "He lived to be 969, the oldest person in the Bible!"

"Except God," Cari piped up from her nest against Mom's arm.

"Right, little chicken." Mom laughed. "Well,

since we aren't to guess, Dad had better tell us."

"Our logging camp is closing down for a time—at least two weeks."

"Really?" Mom looked startled. "What's the problem?"

Dad counted reasons off on his fingers. "We can't go back to work until some of our heavy equipment is replaced. Today we barely avoided a bad accident when a piece failed. The mill had some orders canceled and will be down until after the Fourth of July." He smiled at Mom. "So how would you like to jump in the car and go on vacation? It may be the only time I have off this year."

"Do you have somewhere special in mind?" Mom asked.

Andy held his breath. Their last long vacation seemed forever ago. Last year Mom hadn't been very well. Although Dad had made a great stay-at-home vacation, Andy was more than ready for a trip away from Darrington. Far away, with new and wonderful things to see. ●

5

Alba Church Key

C ari Reynolds popped down from her mother's lap, ran to her father, and crawled onto his knees. "Where are we going? Where are the secrets?"

Dad hugged her and made his voice really deep and mysterious. "Who wants to go to Albuquerque tomorrow?"

"I do!" Cari hollered. Then, "What's an Alba Church Key?"

"It's pronounced Al-buh-kur-key and it's a city in New Mexico," Mom said, her eyes lighting up. "My sister and her family live there. It's been so long since we saw them. Fifteen hundred miles each way is just too far for—"

Andy's mouth fell open. Forgetting his

manners, he interrupted his mother. "You mean we're going to travel *3,000 miles* before we get home?"

"More than that," Dad promised. "As long as we're going that far, we'll stop and see what's along the way. Places like the Grand Canyon and Yellowstone National Park." He grinned at Mom. "Do you think Ned and his family would like to come along? He's off work too."

Andy groaned. "I really love Uncle Ned, but it takes him so long to make up his mind about going places. Your vacation might be over before he decides!"

"It won't." Dad laughed and Mom blinked back happy tears. The Reynoldses had never been to New Mexico. "Ned does consider carefully before saying he will do something. He never makes promises he can't keep."

"Like God promising about the rainbow," Andy said. "Can we, I mean, *may* we go ask him?"

"What about the dishes?" Mom wanted to know. "If we're leaving tomorrow, we'll need to pack when we get home, and dirty dishes don't do themselves."

"Dishes first," Dad said. "If Ned, Hester, and Ellen can go, they'll also need time to pack."

Less than a half hour later the excited family spilled from the car and rushed into Uncle Ned's little brown house on the edge of Darrington. Dad came straight to the point. "We're leaving for Albuquerque tomorrow morning, Ned. Do you and your family want to go with us?"

Tall, lanky Uncle Ned looked surprised. "Hmmm."

Andy rolled his eyes at Mom. She gave him a look that said for him to behave—starting now.

Less than a minute later, he received a shock. Uncle Ned cocked his head to one side and said, "We couldn't go tomorrow. I'd have to change the oil in my car before starting such a long trip. But we could go the next day, if you're willing to wait for us."

Dad nodded. "It's a deal."

"All right!" Andy and Cari cheered.

Two-year-old Ellen clapped her hands and repeated, "All right!" She sounded so much like Cari when she echoed the children that Andy laughed and laughed.

Questions and answers flew back and forth before the Reynoldses headed for home. Andy tumbled from the car, wondering if he'd ever sleep. Everything had happened so fast. Now a trip to "Alba Church Key" (as Cari still called it) was all planned for the day after tomorrow. Even better, Uncle Ned, Auntie Hester, and Cousin Ellen were going with them!

"Thanks, God," Andy said as he ran to help Mom and Dad get ready.

"It's a good thing we had the extra day," Dad said the next evening. Fitting tarpaulins (large sheets of waterproofed canvas used as ground covers to keep beds from getting wet) and blankets for camping out, dishes and pots and pans, food, and four people in the older model Chevrolet meant packing and repacking.

"Put your guitar between you and Cari," Mom told Andy. "My sister and her family will want to hear you play. We can also sing around our campfires at night."

"Don't forget books," Dad advised. "Sometimes we'll be in places without much to see."

"The *World Book Encyclopedias* are too heavy, but we can take our books about animals around the world," Andy told Cari.

"We already have a real, live Andy-mal in the back seat." Cari giggled and Andy made a face.

Dad frowned. "I hope we don't have any car trouble. Ned's Plymouth is older than ours. It would be nice to have a brand-new automobile someday."

"Right, but I still like this one." The boy loyally patted the car that had faithfully carried them around for many years. "We can ask God to help it take us to Albuquerque."

"We certainly will," Dad agreed. "Right now, it's time for bed. Tomorrow morning is going to come mighty early." ●

6

Reporter and Recorder

Andy and Cari didn't think they would sleep the night before they left for New Mexico. They did, but it seemed no time at all before Dad thumped on their bedroom doors and called, "Rise and shine. The sun is peeking over the hill. All aboard the Chevrolet Express to Albuquerque!"

The children leaped out of bed, so excited they found it hard to settle down and eat a good breakfast. By the time the sun had yawned and decided to get on with its job of warming the world, the Reynoldses were at Uncle Ned's. The two families asked God to keep them safe. They thanked Him for His loving care and protection. Then the heavily packed Reynolds Chevrolet started down the road from Darrington to Arlington. Uncle Ned's loaded-down Plymouth followed a safe distance behind. "Just like the caboose on a train," Andy said happily.

Cari sat on a fat pillow so she could see out the window better. "C'boose, c'boose," she echoed. Laughter swept through the car. The trip to Albuquerque had really, truly started.

Mom turned in her seat belt and smiled at the children. "I have a surprise for you."

Andy looked at the trees on both sides of the road. "Already? We just left Darrington."

Cari bounced in her seat belt. "What is it?"

"Each of us has a special job for this trip," Mom told them. "Dad is our driver. I'll be his helper and take over when he gets tired. Also I will be his map reader. He needs someone to help watch for road signs. We'll all do camp chores, but there are two important jobs that need to be done in the car. You're perfect for them. Dad and I even have a title for you: Reynolds and Reynolds, Reporter and Recorder."

She laughed at their expressions of surprise. "Cari, you have sharp eyes. You'll be our special reporter. Every time you see something interesting, be sure to tell us." She reached to the floor beside her and handed Andy a new blank book with lined pages. A sign on the front said "Trip Journal."

"Andy, how would you like to be our recorder?"

"Sure. What do I do?" He ran his finger over the letters on the cover.

"Write down what we see and the things that happen. There are some wonderful sights and experiences ahead of us. We'll take pictures, of course, but there's nothing like the written record of a trip. Next winter when it's all snowy, we can take out our Trip Journal and read it."

"Reading about things is next best to doing them," Dad put in, hands steady on the steering wheel. "Every time we read the Trip Journal, it will be almost like taking our trip all over again." His hearty laugh rang out. "Who knows? Someday you two may read it to your children and grandchildren!"

"I wish we had a Trip Journal of all the stories Grandpa and Grandma used to tell," Andy said when he stopped laughing at the idea of being old enough to have grandchildren.

"Dad 'n' Mom 'n' Uncle Ned have good stories, too," Cari reminded.

"Right. Too bad they aren't written down in a book so more people could know about them," Andy told her.

"Perhaps someday God will direct one or both of you to write such a book," Mom quietly said. "We never can tell what He may have in mind for us."

Andy and Cari looked at each other. It would be so cool if God had them write a book!

"Making a Trip Journal will be good practice, just in case," Andy announced. "Cari, you have to help me a whole bunch. If I'm busy writing, I might miss something important."

"'Course I'll help." Her small chin proudly raised and her eyes looked bluer than the cloudless June sky. "I'm part of Reynolds and Reynolds and whatever else Mom said, aren't I?"

"You sure are." Andy opened the journal. He wrote "Darrington, Washington," and the date in the center of the first page. How clean and white the pages were! By the time the family came home, those pages would be filled with the story of their trip. Andy grinned and added in his very best writing: "Reported by Cari Reynolds. Recorded by Andy Reynolds." He read out loud what he had written. Dad and Mom smiled, but Cari looked prouder than ever to be a special reporter. ●

Water in the Wilderness

7

The two cars took turns leading the way to Albuquerque. The Chevrolet and the Plymouth steadily went up and down little hills. Sometimes the road wound up mountains to high passes. Before they reached the summit they saw patches of snow alongside the road.

"Snow in summer?" Cari stared.

"It's because we're so high up," Andy explained.

On and on they went, climbing higher and higher, until—

"Oh, oh." Dad pointed to a red light on the instrument panel. "Our motor is overheating. We must be low on water." He steered into a parking area. Uncle Ned pulled in behind.

"It's a good thing we brought water with us."

Andy uncurled his legs from where he'd been sitting in the back seat with his guitar between him and Cari. "Want me to fill the radiator?"

"We have to let it cool first." The families didn't mind waiting. Little Ellen laughed and talked to herself. Cari and Andy played in the snow.

"This is the first thing for our Trip Journal," Andy said. "I'll write it down when we get going."

When the radiator had cooled, Dad poured in water. The travelers started out once more. But when the Reynoldses' car chugged up another mountain, the red warning light came back on!

Dad looked worried. "There are no towns for miles. We can use the water Uncle Ned brought, but what will we do after that? Maybe we should go back."

Go back? Andy's high spirits plunged to his toes. Cari looked as if she wanted to cry. "Aren't we going to Alba Church Key?"

"Let's ask the Lord to help us," Mom said. After Dad refilled the radiator, both families gathered in a circle and bowed their heads.

"Heavenly Father," Dad prayed. "The Bible tells us water will gush forth in the wilderness and streams in the desert [Isaiah 35:6]. You know we don't want to give up our trip—unless it's Your will. Please help us. In Jesus' name, Amen."

"Amen," the others added, then Cari demanded, "What's 'gush' and 'wilderness'?"

"I know," Andy proudly said. " 'Gush' means pour out fast. 'Wilderness' is where there aren't any people. Like this." He waved at the huge trees and mountains around them.

"How can God get water here?" Cari asked. "There aren't any rivers or lakes or faucets."

Just then they heard a *chug, chug, chug* as an enormous water truck pulled into the parking turnout. The driver called, "You folks need help?"

"We sure do," Dad told him. The driver filled the radiator and water carriers to the brim.

"We asked God for water and He sent you," Cari told the good-natured man.

He looked startled. "It wouldn't surprise me." He drove away smiling.

God answered the travelers' prayers several more times before Dad could get the car fixed. "In funny ways," Andy said while he watched Dad pour the last of their breakfast drink in the radiator! "I can hardly wait to write about this in our Trip Journal."

"It will get us off the mountain and down into the valley," Mom reminded him.

"What then?" Cari asked.

Dad smiled at her in the rearview mirror. "We'll just have to trust the Lord."

Down they rolled. Andy suddenly sat up, straight as if someone had put a snowball down his back. He rubbed his eyes. "What is *that?*" He pointed to something white shooting up in the air along the road. It looked like a big water fountain.

Dad sighed with relief. "I can't believe it. Thank God. An artesian well, just when we need one."

The children stared at the great fountain gushing high into the air. Once more, God had provided water.

The next time water ran low, they were on a hilltop. "We can coast down," Dad said. "The radiator will cool and not use so much water." To their surprise, a tiny service station sat at the bottom of the hill, although nothing had been marked on their map! The owner fixed the radiator enough so they could make it to a city and have a new one put in.

"Write these things down, Andy," Dad said when the mechanic had finished his work. "We don't want to forget them. Although we may not see another water truck or artesian well, God knew what we needed."

"He really did make water that gushed, didn't He, Dad?" Cari asked.

"Right. Everyone back in the car. Albuquerque, here we come." ●

Author's Note: Dad was right. In their travels that year and many other years, the family never saw another water truck or artesian well.

What did God do
for the kangaroo?

8

For the Kangaroo Too?

Andy put down his Trip Journal and pencil. "Hey, Dad. You said we'd see a lot of new secrets on our trip. Was the artesian well a secret?"

"And the water truck?" Cari added.

"The water truck was a blessing," Dad said. "Some people would call it a coincidence. We know better. There's not much chance it would be there exactly when and where we needed it."

"The artesian well is one of God's secrets," Mom added. "He created water under pressure in the earth. People bore down to it, and the water shoots up like a fountain."

"Artesian wells look kind of like geysers," Andy said.

Cari asked curiously, "What's that?"

Mom took out a map of Wyoming. "Here's a picture of a geyser we'll see."

"That's Old Faithful in Yellowstone Park," Andy said.

Cari stared at the picture of steaming, leaping water. "It looks like a hot ar-teasing well."

"Artesian wells gush up into the air," Mom said gently. "So do geysers, but they are boiling hot. Besides, people don't have to dig holes for the water to rush out. It pushes its own way up through the ground."

Cari's eyes grew wide. "It comes all by itself?"

"All by itself, and often at regular times."

"That is so neat—" Andy broke off. "Look, Cari! Quick!" He pointed out the window on her side of the car. An animal with enormous ears sat by the side of the road, staring at them with big eyes. Suddenly the brownish-gray creature bounded away. Its stubby white tail looked like a little flag. It disappeared behind a huge clump of grayish-green plants Dad said was sagebrush. Their father pulled off to the side of the road. Uncle Ned followed in his car.

"What is it?" Cari squealed. "A deer? It ran so fast!"

Dad laughed. "It's a jackrabbit. You're right. It is a really fast runner. Now you know why people say things happen quicker than a jackrabbit."

The animal hopped out from behind the sagebrush. The children had never seen such a big rabbit. It must have been two feet long. "Did God make the back legs long so jackrabbits could hop fast and get away from danger?"

"Yes. God did all kinds of special things for the animals. Just like He does special things for us." Mom's laughter bubbled over. "Every time I see a jackrabbit, I think of a kangaroo. They hop ever faster than jackrabbits, but using only their back legs."

"I want to see a kangaroo," Cari announced. "Is that one?" She pointed toward a second animal some distance from the road.

"No. It's another jackrabbit. Kangaroos don't live in America. They live across the ocean, mostly in Australia," Andy told her. She looked disappointed, so he took out a book on animals. "I'll see if I can find a picture."

"What did God do for the kangaroo?" Cari asked.

Andy found a picture and description of kangaroos. Cari looked at it. Her mouth dropped open. "There's a little kangaroo's head sticking out of the big one's middle! Is it getting born?"

"No. Baby kangaroos are only an inch long when they are born. They're called *joeys*. Their mothers carry them in a pouch—that's like a built-in purse on their stomachs—until the joeys are 6 or 8 months old. That way, nothing can hurt them."

Cari traced the picture with her finger. "How fast does God make them hop?"

"The book says up to 40 miles an hour. They can also leap six feet in the air."

"Joey Kangaroo and his mama have big ears like Jack Rabbit's, but Jack doesn't have a long tail," Cari pointed out.

Andy grinned. He didn't bother to tell his sister the animals were *joeys* and *jackrabbits*, not Joey Kangaroo and Jack Rabbit. "Our animal book says the big ears are so they can flip them from front to back to hear danger and hop away. The powerful tail is for balance when they walk or stand up."

"What did God do for other animals, Andy?"

"Better save your book for the long, empty stretches," Dad advised. "Otherwise, you'll miss what's happening right now. Such as those two jackrabbits playing tag."

Cari pressed her nose to the window. After a long time, she said, "I made a poem.

"What did God do for the kangaroo?
And for the other animals, too?"

"That's a good poem," Andy said. "I'm going to write in the back of our Trip Journal the things God did for the animals. When we get home, I'll make another poster like we did when Mom was sick." ●

9

"Bearly" Awake

Now that the radiator didn't leak all the water, the two families headed for Yellowstone Park. Cari's and Andy's eyes opened wide at the things they saw. When she spotted the pools of bubbling, colored mud called Paint Pots, she made a face. The smell stung her nose.

She and Andy liked Old Faithful Geyser better. "The water erupts, which means rushes from the ground because of pressure," the park ranger explained. "It often shoots 100 feet high." A low rumbling began. "Right on time," the ranger shouted above the noise. A great flood of boiling water exploded into the air. Higher and higher it went. The Reynoldses and Uncle Ned's family stayed back where it was safe and watched until

God's natural water show ended. Cari begged to stay and see it again.

"Sorry, honey," Dad said. "It won't erupt again for about an hour. We have much more to see."

"What, Dad?" she asked as she climbed back in the car. The others followed.

"Give us a hint," Andy teased.

Dad chuckled. "Some are mentioned in a song we sang around the campfire last night."

"That was fun," Cari said.

"Right." Andy remembered how some of the people camped nearby joined in the singing while he played his guitar. Now if he could remember all the songs— "I know!" He started singing "Home on the Range."

"Are we really going to see buffaloes roam and bears and ant'lopes play?" Cari interrupted.

"That's deer and antelope," Mom told her. "We probably won't see any bears."

"How come, Mom?" Andy wanted to know. "It seems like a good place for them." He looked out the car window at rolling meadows, silvery streams, and tall, forest-covered mountains.

"There were many bears until foolish people disobeyed the warning signs not to feed them. Some teased the bears until they were no longer safe. People got hurt, so the bears had to go."

Andy felt sad. "That's not fair. This was their home first!"

"I know." Dad chuckled again. "Mom and I remember something about Yellowstone bears."

"We sure do!" Their mother rolled her eyes. "Dad and I camped here years ago. We strung a tarpaulin over a rope between two trees and tied down the edges for a shelter. Early the next morning I heard a grunting sound. I opened my eyes and saw a furry brown head in the opening of the tent. *Two dark eyes stared in at me.*"

Cari gasped.

"What did you *do?*" Andy blurted.

"I screamed *bear* and jumped out of my blankets. Dad sat up and hollered, 'Boo, bear!'"

Mom laughed so hard she couldn't go on.

Dad finished the story. "It scared the curious bear so much he went *thud, thud, thud* on his big paws and got away from us as fast as he could."

"Boo, bear," Cari cried. "Boo!"

"God took care of us," Dad added. "People can get hurt by wild animals."

"What did God do for bears?" Cari clapped her hands and looked proud of herself. "Oh. I remember. They can't find food in winter, so He makes them hi-bear-nate, which means sleep."

"You're smart to remember that," Andy told her. "But it's hi-*ber*-nate, not hi-*bear*-nate." He dug out the animal book. "That's not all God did for bears. He taught them to eat all the food they can in the fall and get fat. Some bears, especially in the far north, also stuff their stomachs with spruce or balsam needles before hibernating. Hey, listen to this! Frogs and snakes and lizards and turtles and chipmunks also hibernate in cold weather. Neat."

Andy read on. "That's not all. Some bats sleep during the day and come out at night. Hummingbirds do just the opposite. They sleep nights and are active during the day."

"Like us," Cari said. She squealed. "Look! A whole lot of great big shaggy somethings!"

"Those are buffalo, also called *bison,*" Mom explained. The family watched the herd of brownish-black bison, who stared back at them. Cari loved the small, yellowish-red buffalo calves that Dad said had been born in May or June. "The bull who leads the herd helps the mother cows defend their young from enemies," he explained. He rolled down the window and took pictures from where it was safe.

"Like you help Mom take care of us," Andy said. When they could no longer see the herd, he turned to the back of the Trip Journal. He carefully wrote down what God did for buffaloes and bears, and the other creatures they had learned about that day. ●

A Prairie Dog Town

10

Changing Colors

Before the travelers left Yellowstone Park, they saw both deer and antelope. Andy and Cari thrilled when something startled the herd and the graceful animals leaped away. "Just like Jack Rabbit and Joey Kangaroo," Cari said. "Did God make their legs long so they can hurry?"

"Yes," Dad replied. "He also made other creatures with long, strong legs."

Andy grinned. "I wish mine were longer and stronger when I run down the soccer field!" He thought for a moment. "Horses use their legs to carry riders and run fast."

Cari flipped through the pages of the animal book. "Frogs hop on their long back legs."

"Dogs don't hop, but they run fast," Andy

said. "Cari, do you know some dogs have jobs?"

"Really? Just like people?" She sat up straight. "Who is their boss? God?"

Andy grinned. "Sort of. I mean, He gave them a great sense of smell. Trained dogs help police officers find hidden drugs by sniffing them out. Other dogs help herd sheep. In snowy countries, dogs find and carry medicine to lost and hurt travelers."

"Speaking of dogs, look out the window," Dad told them.

"I don't see any dogs," Andy said. "I don't see anything."

"I don't either," Cari added.

"Roll your windows down and look more closely." Dad guided the car to the side of the road. The ground beyond the parking lot suddenly came alive with furry tan animals sitting up like an army of people. *Bark. Bark. Bark.* Before the sound stopped echoing, the animals vanished into hundreds of holes in the ground!

"It sounded like dogs barking, Dad. What are they? Why didn't we see them before?"

"They're called prairie dogs, because of their warning call. You didn't see them, because God created them to blend into where they live."

"May we get out of the car?" Cari asked.

"Yes. Then stand perfectly still and see what happens."

The children obeyed. Uncle Ned, Auntie Hester, and Cousin Ellen left their car, too. Everyone stood quietly. In a moment a furry brown head popped out of the ground. Then another, and another, until they saw too many prairie dogs to count. "They live underground in burrows called prairie dog towns," Dad whispered. "One town may have 500 prairie dogs!"

The families watched the prairie dogs chase each other and pop in and out of holes for a long time. That night around the campfire, they talked about the interesting animals.

Uncle Ned smiled when Cari said God made the prairie dogs the same color as where they lived. "Do you know God also made animals that change colors for protection against enemies?" he asked her.

"Like a rainbow?" Her blue eyes sparkled and Andy leaned forward to hear better. Uncle Ned knew a great deal about animals. Not just those near Darrington, but from faraway lands.

Now their logger uncle laughed. "No. They become the color of their surroundings."

Andy scooted closer to Uncle Ned. "What are some of them?"

"Ptarmigans *(tar-muh-guns)* are grouse-like birds that live in Alaska and other cold places. Their summer coats of reddish-brown and black turn snowy white in winter. They have short feathers on their feet to help them travel across the snow. Other creatures in the north countries also turn white in winter. Ermines, which are weasels, have short, silky brown hair in summer. Arctic hares, sometimes called snowshoe rabbits, also become white in winter to match the snow and ice."

"Tell us s'more," Cari begged when he paused for a moment.

"Please," Andy added. He loved learning what God did for the animals He had created.

Uncle Ned mysteriously lowered his voice. "One of the strangest things people in the North see in winter—actually what they *don't* see—is the shadow fox." He chuckled. So did Auntie Hester. Ellen clapped her hands and laughed, too.

Andy smiled at his little cousin. She was too small to understand her father's stories. She just liked to laugh when the others did. Then, puzzled by Uncle Ned's tale, Andy quickly asked, "What is a shadow fox? How can people not see it and still know it's there?"

His uncle's eyes gleamed. "When the sun shines on the snow, travelers sometimes see a shadow. They must look really hard to even see three dark dots: the arctic fox's eyes and nose."

"When we get home, you can find pictures

in our *World Book* under animals of the polar regions." Dad yawned. "Right now, let's thank God for taking care of us, then get to bed." ●

Out popped
a tiny striped chipmunk.

11

Secret of the Bread Sack

The travelers headed east from Yellowstone Park. They crossed Wyoming on their way to South Dakota. "We'll camp at Devils Tower National Monument tonight," Dad told his family. He pointed to an enormous rock in the distance. Although the family had first seen it hours earlier, it didn't ever seem to be any closer.

Cari crossed her arms and said flatly, "I don't want to stay there."

"Why not? If there's a trail, we can climb it," Andy told her. "Well, partway. It's pretty tall."

Dad laughed. "You're right about that! There is a trail around the bottom, but it takes a lot more skill and equipment than we have to climb the rock. Cari, why don't you want to stay here?"

She looked worried. "God won't like it. We asked Him to come with us on our trip. He won't stay at the devil's tower. I don't want to, either."

Mom frowned in the rearview mirror at Andy, who had started laughing. "It's just a name, honey. The devil didn't make the big rock, and he isn't there. It's God's rock, not the devil's."

"Honest?" Cari still sounded doubtful.

"Honest. Look, there are even more prairie dogs than we saw before!"

"This is one of the largest prairie dog towns anywhere," Dad said. He drove onto the shoulder of the road so they could watch the hundreds of strange creatures that looked like huge squirrels.

Cari forgot all about Devils Tower. "They are so *cute!*"

Another car pulled up behind them. Someone honked a horn. *Bark. Bark. Bark.* The warning signal sounded, and the prairie dogs dived into their holes. When everything grew quiet, heads peeped out of the ground and back came the prairie dogs to sit on their hind legs and stare curiously at the cars.

"I bet God had fun making prairie dogs," Cari said.

"He must have," Andy told her. "He sure made a lot of them!"

A few hours later something mysterious happened. After supper and a long walk around the base of Devils Tower, Andy brought out his guitar. The two families began to sing. Suddenly Cari's eyes opened wide. She pointed to the picnic table, where the supper supplies still lay.

Everyone turned in the direction of her pointing finger. Andy gasped. *The bread sack was slowly moving across the table.*

"Is it magic?" Cari whispered.

"M'jik?" little Ellen echoed.

The corners of Auntie Hester's mouth curled in a smile. "You know we don't believe in magic. Shh. Be still and listen."

"Shh," Ellen repeated, putting her fingers over her mouth.

The sack moved again. "Does the sack have a secret?" Cari whispered loud enough for everyone to hear. "I never saw a bread sack *walk* before."

The sack did look as if it were walking across the picnic table. Andy knew it couldn't, but he still kept his attention on the moving object.

Rustle. Rustle. Rustle. The sack stopped. Andy held his breath. Out popped a tiny striped chipmunk. The piece of brown bread in its mouth looked almost as big as the chipmunk itself! The animal cocked its head to one side and watched them with shiny bright eyes. When Andy and the others began laughing, away the chipmunk went, carrying its stolen dinner.

Songs forgotten, the children took turns breaking bread from the loaf they now couldn't use and throwing it to the many chipmunks who came for a handout. "Don't try to get them to eat from your hands," Mom warned. "They may seem tame, but they're still wild animals and can bite. God gave them sharp teeth so they can crack nuts."

"I love how they sit up and hold their food in their front paws." Cari spread her open hands wide. "Sorry, chipmunks. It's all gone."

The furry little creatures chattered, then ran across the ground searching for crumbs. Their tails switched back and forth like windshield wipers on the car when rain poured down.

After the chipmunks whisked away, Andy ran to the car for the Trip Journal. "There was so much to see today, I forgot to write it down," he said. He laughed and started writing. "I'm going to call this part 'Secret of the Bread Sack.' Cari, you can draw a picture of a chipmunk to put in the journal. OK?"

"Tomorrow," she mumbled. Her eyes closed. "I'm awake but my eyes are asleep."

"Ellen's eyes 'sleep," their girl cousin repeated. She tumbled into her mother's lap, and another exciting day of their wonderful trip came to a close. ●

Funny Faces

One night the Reynoldses and Uncle Ned's family camped beside a lake. The wind was so strong that they wondered if they would be blown away. "Funny," Andy said. "Washington wind sounds friendlier than South Dakota wind!"

Another afternoon they chose a campsite, then left to explore for a few hours. When they returned, the outhouse (outdoor bathroom) near their campsite had disappeared!

"Where did it go?" Cari demanded.

"I don't know," her brother said after they searched the area. "Maybe the park rangers moved it." The families ended up using another outhouse a little ways off. Andy laughed and wrote in the Trip Journal: "Mystery of the Missing Outhouse,"

SOTC-3

page **65**

then recorded what happened. "If weird things keep happening, maybe someday I'll write a mystery story about them!" he said to himself.

At Mount Rushmore National Memorial the families arrived in the afternoon and stayed until it got dark, so they could see the mountainside lighted.

Dad and Uncle Ned took off their hats when they gazed up at the four faces carved into the granite. Andy's and Cari's mouths dropped open. Even from a distance the faces looked *so big!*

"Who are they?" Cari asked.

Andy felt proud that he knew the answer to her question. "George Washington, who is called the Father of our Country because he was the first president. Abraham Lincoln, who helped free the slaves. Thomas Jefferson and Theodore 'Teddy' Roosevelt, both great Americans and important presidents."

"Is that what God did for the mountain?" Cari wanted to know. "Put faces on it?"

Andy shook his head and bit his lip to keep from laughing. "No. People did it. It took more than 14 years. I read that George Washington's head is 60 feet tall, as high as a five-story building!"

Cari looked surprised. "How tall is that?"

"About three times as tall as any building in Darrington," Andy explained.

"Oh." She stared at the faces some more. "Maybe someone will carve our faces on a mountain someday."

"Probably not, but our names are already written in a Book," Dad said.

"Right." Andy grinned. "Our Trip Journal."

His father smiled back at him. "Yes, but that's not the Book I mean. When you asked Jesus to live in your hearts and promised to follow Him, your names went into the book of life. Remember what Jesus said in John 3:16?"

"Yes," the children chorused. "'For God so loved the world, that he gave his only begotten Son, that whosoever believeth in him should not perish, but have everlasting life.'"

"It's nice to see our presidents honored here," Mom said. "But it's far more important for us and everyone to be listed in the book of life."

Cari stared at the stone faces. "Are they?"

"We can't know that for sure," Dad quietly said. "We do know the word *whosoever* means all who believe. History tells us many of our presidents were godly men. They prayed and tried to lead the country according to God's will."

Just then the sky turned black. Rain swept across the hills. Great drops pounded the earth. Everyone rushed inside the covered area to hear the park ranger talk. He told them, "Keep your eyes turned toward the mountain. In a moment I'll turn on the floodlights. I promise you'll see something you will never forget."

He flipped the switch. No one moved. No one spoke. Then a small boy yelled, "Hey, Mom! Mr. Lincoln's wearing a stocking cap!"

The crowd howled with laughter. Because of the heavy rain pouring down over them the presidents' faces looked as if they were wearing strange masks. Waterfalls hung from George Washington's eyebrows. Abraham Lincoln really did look like he had on a stocking cap.

"The ranger said we'd never forget this." Dad laughed until tears came. So did the others.

The laughter died down when they got in the cars and started down the steep and winding road to their campsite. The rain had stopped, but heavy fog lay just above the road, making it almost impossible to see. "It's like driving into a white blanket," Andy said.

Dad nodded and kept the car at the slowest speed possible. Uncle Ned's headlights behind them looked like two tiny sparks.

"Please take care of us, God," Mom prayed. Dad and the children all said, "Amen."

Mile after anxious mile passed. At last they reached their camp. They all agreed none of them would ever forget Mount Rushmore, the missing outhouse, or the funny mountain faces. Most of all, they would remember how God brought them through the terrible fog and back to their camp. ●

Hundreds of sheep blocked
the way, bells tinkling.

13

One, Two, Three Parades?

A ndy Reynolds watched the wide spaces out the window of the car. The Wyoming flatlands and rolling hills seemed to go on forever. "This sure is different than Darrington," he said.

"It sure is," Cari echoed. "Why did all the mountains move away?"

Andy turned his head so she wouldn't see him laugh. "There weren't any. It's just different here."

"I know." Suddenly she squealed. "Even the butterflies are different!" The family stared at a great blue cloud dipping and floating across the dry ground. None of them had ever seen butterflies the color of the sky.

"Did God do anything special for butterflies?" Cari asked.

"Yes." Andy grabbed a book and opened it. He showed Cari a picture.

"That's not a butterfly. That's a creepy caterpillar."

"It will be a butterfly." Andy pointed to another picture. A beautiful butterfly was crawling out of a sacklike shell. "It's called a cocoon," Andy explained. "Butterflies are fragile, which means delicate and weak. The *pupa,* which we usually call a cocoon, protects the butterfly until it is strong enough to break free and fly." He turned the page. "The book says there are between 15,000 and 20,000 kinds of butterflies. Some are less than one-half inch from wingtip to wingtip. One in New Guinea is 11 inches wide!" Her brother held his hands apart to show Cari how big that was.

"Butterflies are like chickens," Cari surprised everyone by saying. "They come out of a shell."

A little later an unpleasant odor crept into the car. "Yuck." Cari grabbed her nose.

So did Andy. "Do you remember what God did for skunks?" he asked his sister.

She let go of her nose and mumbled, "He made them smell terrible to protect them."

"Good girl," Dad told her. "Uh-oh. Looks like we're going to be held up."

The children peered out the window. "It's a parade," Cari cried. "We're in a buffalo parade!"

Indeed they were. The shaggy beasts soon surrounded the cars. Dad and Uncle Ned slowed until they barely crawled along. At last they got through the buffalo herd. Later, they ended up in another "parade." Hundreds of sheep blocked the way, bells tinkling. Again the travelers had to drive slowly. They enjoyed watching the skillful sheep-dogs round up the animals that wandered away.

"One parade, two parades," Cari chanted. "What's next, Dad?"

He laughed and shook his head. "I can't imagine!"

"Another parade, maybe?" But Andy didn't really believe it.

Late that afternoon they came to Evanston in southwestern Wyoming. Dad rolled down the window. Band music floated into the car. "I wonder what's going on?" He turned right at a stop sign. Uncle Ned followed. Crowds of cheering people lined both sides of the wide street.

"Why is everyone smiling and waving?" Cari asked, eyes as blue as the butterflies they'd seen earlier.

A chuckle started at Dad's toes and worked its way up. He pointed to brightly decorated floats and bands ahead of them. Checking the rearview mirror, he said, "There are more behind Ned's car. Andy, Cari, we're in the middle of another parade, a real one this time!"

More people waved and laughed. "We can turn off at the next corner," Mom suggested.

Dad chuckled again. "Sorry. The street's blocked off." The two dusty cars with Washington State license plates stayed in the middle of the Evanston, Wyoming, parade all the way to the edge of town.

"One, two, three parades," Cari sang. "This is so fun!"

That day's adventures weren't over. Heavy rain fell again. Dad said they couldn't make camp without getting soaked. Yet all the motels said "No Vacancy." Darkness came. Miles lay between them and another town. To make things worse, Uncle Ned's car lights began acting up.

"We'll have to find a good place to pull off the road and sleep in the car," Dad said after talking to Uncle Ned. "I don't like to do it, but it's safer than trying to go on. We'll just trust God to take care of us."

Andy's stomach rumbled like the geysers in Yellowstone Park. "What about supper?"

"Too wet for a fire. We'll have to make do with leftovers." The boy wanted to laugh when Dad asked the blessing over supper: leftover potato salad made into sandwiches! He grinned and said, "We're better off than Ned and his family. They're eating leftover *baked bean* sandwiches."

Four people and a guitar crowded into a car made sleeping hard. When they awakened, they found themselves surrounded once more—with fields of green beans! Andy wrote in the Trip Journal: "I don't think any of us will ever forget sleeping in the car on what Dad nicknamed 'Bean Hill.' We're just glad God took care of us. No one bothered us at all. We probably won't ever eat potato salad sandwiches again, but we were so hungry last night, even they tasted good!" ●

14

What Did God Do . . . ?

O ne afternoon Andy looked around their campsite. "Most cities don't let you camp in their parks. I'm glad this one does. It's nice." He broke off. "My goodness, what is *that?*"

Grrrowl. Roar. Yip, yip.

"The City Park must be near a zoo," Mom suggested. "Let's walk over and see the animals."

Cari danced up and down and sang the song she'd made up, but changed some of the words.

"What did God do for the kangaroo?
And all the animals at the zoo?"

Then she quickly added, "Will there be a kangaroo?"

"I don't think so," Mom said. "The zoo is probably too small to have kangaroos."

"Not like Woodland Park in Seattle." Andy remembered the family trip to the huge zoo. It had so many animals Cari had said she needed an extra pair of eyes to see them all!

Grrrowl. Roar. Yip, yip.

Cari clung to her mother's hand. "Why are the zoo people so noisy?"

"They aren't zoo people. They're zoo animals," Andy told her. "We're people."

"People," little Ellen chirped from her position on her tall father's shoulder.

Soon the families reached a large, heavily screened area. Two cougars (mountain lions) lay soaking up the sun. Now and then one yawned and roared. "They look like big pussycats, but they don't sound like them!" Cari said, keeping a tight hold on Dad's hand.

"God gives lions their roar to frighten enemies, including people who hunt them," Dad said.

Cari pointed to a cage with yellowish-brown animals. "Why did they put the dogs in a cage?"

"They are coyotes *(ky oh tees),* not dogs." Uncle Ned smiled at the little girl.

She didn't look convinced. "They sound like dogs."

Uncle Ned chuckled. "They also howl, especially evenings, nights, and early mornings. Do you know coyotes and wolves can call their family and friends long distance?"

Cari's eyes opened wide. "I don't see any telephones."

Everyone laughed and Ned continued. "They don't need phones. Instead, they point their noses to the sky and howl. The sound carries across the open range, into the valleys, and over the hills."

The next cage held a brownish-black bear, pacing back and forth. "I like seeing animals, but I feel sorry for the bear," Andy said. "I'll bet it wishes it could be out catching fish for its dinner."

The bear swung its head and growled low in its throat. Then it sat down, put its nose on its paws, and lay still. It made Andy sad. Being cooped up in a cage, even a big one, couldn't be fun.

Cari giggled when they came to a father, mother, and baby elephant. "The baby's skin is so loose and gray and wrinkled, it looks old!" she said. "It looks tough, too."

Dad shook his head. "It actually isn't, Cari. It's so tender that mosquitoes and flies can bite into it. That's why God gave elephants ropelike tails. They use them to switch off insects."

"Like our neighbors' cows and horses," Cari put in.

"Cows 'n' horses," Ellen faithfully echoed.

"How come elephants have such long noses?" Cari wanted to know.

"They're called trunks," Andy answered. "Elephants breathe, sniff, and smell with them."

"That's not all." Auntie Hester's eyes sparkled. "Watch and see what else trunks are like."

The mother elephant stretched her trunk toward the ground. She scooped up a pile of freshly cut grass and stuffed it into her mouth. "A hand!" Cari cried. "Her trunk is like a hand."

The baby elephant put the end of its trunk into a huge tub of water and sucked. It shot the water into its mouth, then refilled its trunk. "It's like a pitcher," Andy said. "And a shower." He ducked when the baby elephant filled its trunk and shot a stream of water over itself!

"An adult elephant can carry one and a half gallons of water in its trunk," Uncle Ned said.

Andy blinked. "Really? Then the trunk is like the radiator on our car."

"Do other animals have ray-dee-ate-ors?" Cari asked after they went back to their campsite.

"Camels don't need to carry water. They go across deserts with very little to drink. But they have a cupboard, though." Andy grinned and ran for his animal book. "Look!" He pointed to the humps in the pictures. "Some people think camels carry water in the humps. They don't. Humps are big, huge lumps of fat. They give the camels energy when they can't find food."

That evening Cari added a new verse to her little song.

"What did God do for the kangaroo?
And all the animals at the zoo?
Camels have cupboards without any water.
Elephants' trunks are like car ray-dee-ate-ors." ●

Noises in the Night

15

Cari snuggled farther down in her sleeping bag to drown out the scary noises in the night.

It didn't help much. *Grrrowl. Roar. Yip, yip.* Cari shivered with fear. She poked her brother and said, "Andy, are you awake?"

"We all are." A loud blast of animal sounds followed Dad's calm voice.

His daughter gulped. "Did someone let the zoo people out of their cages? Are they going to eat us?"

"No," Mom said firmly.

Andy felt laughter bubble up inside him until it spilled out. "Next time we camp in a city park let's make sure it isn't next to a zoo!"

Cari felt better when everybody laughed, but

nobody got much sleep that night. As soon as daylight came, they hurriedly fixed breakfast, packed, and left. "No more night noises," Andy said with an enormous yawn.

His prediction proved wrong. During the middle of the next night he heard someone laughing, followed by the sound of chewing. Andy raised up on one elbow. Mom and Cari lay fast asleep. Dad's even breathing said he also slept. *Should I check it out?* Andy wondered. He shook his head. No way was he going to leave his family and try to identify some strange noise.

The sounds grew louder. Finally, Dad crawled out of bed.

Cari awakened and whispered, "Who is laughing?"

"Come see," Dad said mysteriously. Mom and the children scrambled to where he stood. Bright moonlight shone on two lumpy-looking, waddling creatures that chuckled as they moved.

"Porcupines," Dad said. "They won't hurt us if we don't bother them. Let's go back to bed."

The family fell asleep to the now-friendly sound of the porcupines chuckling. But the next morning they found sharp teeth marks on two of the metal drinking cups! After breakfast Andy showed Cari a picture of a porcupine, all covered with sharp needle-like quills. "Porcupines don't shoot their quills at their enemies," he explained. "They strike attackers with their quilled tails. The quills come out and stick in the enemies, then new quills grow back in the tail."

Uncle Ned then told them something not in the animal book. "Many people who live in the snowy far north never kill porcupines unless they are starving. The animals move so slowly it is easy to catch them." He made a face. "The meat is supposed to taste terrible, but trappers and others who got caught out in winter tell stories of how eating porcupines saved their lives."

Andy stared at the sharp quills in the picture. "Those quills are better than armor," he said. Cari looked puzzled, so he explained. "Armor is a suit of metal clothes that protects whoever wears it. People wore armor in the olden days when they marched into battle."

Mom smiled at the children. "We have a secret protection that is far better than quills or metal clothing," she said. "It not only protects against enemies, but against evil!"

"What is it?" Cari shouted. "Is it sharper than Porky Pine's quills?"

"The apostle Paul tells about it in his letter to the Ephesians," Mom replied. "Bring me a Bible from the car, please."

When Cari returned with it Mom opened the

Bible to Ephesians 6. "Verses 10-17 tell us to be strong in the Lord and in His mighty power. Paul says to put on the whole armor of God so we can stand against the devil's schemes." She went on to list all the parts of the armor and explained each.

Truth: a belt to be buckled around the waist

Righteousness: a breastplate (covering) for the upper body

The gospel of peace (Jesus' teachings): shoes, to be worn by those who love the Lord

Faith: a shield so strong it can put out flaming arrows of evil

Salvation: a helmet, better than any bicycle safety helmet

The word of God: a sword of His Spirit, stronger than any earthly weapon

Prayer: for all occasions

"I never knew that was in the Bible," Cari blurted out.

"There are more secrets and mysteries and wonders in this one Book than anyone on earth can solve," Dad said. "When Jesus comes back for His followers, we will know the answers to them."

"Really?" Cari sounded excited.

"Really. Jesus told His disciples in both Matthew and Luke the knowledge of the secrets of the kingdom of heaven had been given to them and even more would follow."*

Andy shot his fists into the air. "Yes!" He grinned. "Those are sure great secrets."

"In the meantime, we can continue to enjoy discovering those in our own world," Auntie Hester reminded. "Not a day goes by without my learning something new about God's goodness and being thankful for this wonderful, amazing world."

"If we're going to see any more of this wonderful, amazing world, we'd best get a move on," Uncle Ned teased.

Little Ellen clapped her hands. "Move on. Move on." Her mother scooped her up, and the others ran to get ready for another day. ●

---

*Matthew 13:11, 12 and Luke 8:9

A Gazillion Grasshoppers

16

T oday has been bird day," Andy wrote in the Trip Journal several hours later. Indeed it had. The travelers had seen birds of many sizes: hummingbirds, whose sound and name came from the incredibly rapid beat of their tiny wings. Eagles, blessed with powerful wings and keen eyesight that allowed them to fly high and swoop to earth after food. Hawks, which had such wonderful vision they could spot small mice scampering far below.

When the country through which they traveled became flat and seemingly birdless, Andy and Cari took out their books. Cari turned to the picture of a seagull, like those that lived near Puget Sound in Washington. "Why aren't there seagulls here?"

Andy burst into laughter. "There's no sea here. No sea. No seagulls. Get it?"

"Oh." Cari laughed along with him.

Dad said in his I-know-a-secret voice, "Would you like to hear a story about seagulls? It actually happened, and is recorded in history books and encyclopedias."

The children loved Dad's stories. "Tell us, Dad. Please," they teased.

"One of the things the early settlers in the West most feared and dreaded was grasshoppers," Dad began. "Some years swarms were so thick they hid the sun and darkened the sky. Settlers could hear the insects' powerful jaws and sharp teeth crunching. The pests ate every plant, every blade of grass. The grasshoppers covered everything. If doors and windows had cracks around them, they even came in the houses!"

"Yeccch!" Cari made a horrible face.

"That wasn't all," Dad went on. "The grasshoppers laid millions of eggs in the ground. The young hatched the next spring, were full grown by summer, and attacked the crops again. In those days farmers didn't have any way to stop them."

Andy squinted at the brilliantly shining sun. "Wow! There must have been a gazillion grasshoppers to blot out all that light."

"There were," Dad said quietly. "In 1848

great waves of grasshoppers came. The settlers tried to beat them off, but there were too many. The only hope of saving crops and having food to eat was in prayer. The settlers prayed to God, asking Him to save them from the plague, which means anything that sweeps through and does terrible damage."

"Did He?" Cari and Andy shouted together.

"Yes, and in a way no one could have imagined in their wildest dreams! Great flocks of seagulls flew into the area. They ate every single grasshopper before they could destroy the crops. Not one was left to lay eggs in the ground."

"Did God send the seagulls?" Cari asked, eyes wide with excitement.

"He must have," Andy told her. "The ocean was hundreds of miles away."

Cari stared at the seagull in the book. "So there were seagulls, but no sea."

"Right." Andy closed his eyes partway and thought about the miracle of the seagulls. "It's neat that God cared enough to send all those birds far away from home to help the people," he finally said. His eyes popped wide open. "Hey! It's kind of like Jesus being born, isn't it?"

Cari shook her head. "I don't understand."

"Sure you do. God sent the seagulls all those miles to help the settlers. But He sent Jesus clear from heaven, a lot farther away than Washington."

"That's right, son," Dad said. "We should be thankful for it every moment of our lives."

"I'm going to write the story in our Trip Journal," Andy announced. "We don't ever want to forget it." He laughed. "Maybe I'll call it 'God and the Grasshoppers!'"

During lunch break, Andy and Cari walked around the roadside rest area. Cari pointed to an insect. "Is that a hopper grass?" the little girl wanted to know.

"Grasshopper," Andy corrected. "Yes. There's another."

Cari looked at the sun and grabbed her big brother's hand. "Are more coming? Will God have to send the seagulls again?"

"I don't think so." A funny little feeling went through Andy. He didn't let Cari know about it. It would only frighten her. He wondered how the settlers felt when they saw millions of insects blackening the sky. They must have rejoiced and thanked God when the seagulls came!

Cari dropped his hand and ran toward Mom, but Andy looked into the sky and whispered, "I'll never see a grasshopper without remembering Dad's story, God. I'm glad we don't have plagues of them now. Thanks for sending the seagulls. And Jesus." He hurried after his sister. ●

The lynx crouched
on a rock, ready to spring.

Good Samaritans

17

The travelers couldn't always find a church, so sometimes they made camp, stayed over a day, and held their own worship service. Sam played his guitar and they sang hymns. Other campers sometimes joined in. The Reynolds family told Bible stories. Everyone loved the story of the good Samaritan, who helped a hurt Jewish man, even though Samaritans and Jews hated each other.

"Jesus wants us to help out when we can," Auntie Hester said. "Like the good Samaritan."

"Good American," Ellen said. She looked surprised when everyone laughed, but Uncle Ned said, "That, too! God expects us to uphold the laws of our country, as long as they are godly."

One day in the beautiful Colorado mountains

Dad rounded a sharp turn in the winding road, braked hard, and pulled to the side. His sharp eyes had spotted something important. "Look!" He pointed to a large, catlike animal crouched on a big rock, ready to spring. Just below, a spotted fawn (baby deer) stood, obviously unaware of danger.

"It's a lynx," Dad cried. "Slam the car doors and yell as loud as you can!"

The family spilled from the car and screamed. Dad picked up a large rock and threw it toward the lynx. The rock clattered against the stony hillside. The fawn leaped down the rocky ledge at the first sound of noise. Its strong legs carried it away from danger. The lynx turned toward the travelers, spitting and snarling. Little tufts on its ears stood straight up. Cari shivered, but the lynx was too far away to hurt them. Everyone yelled again. Dad fired off another rock. The lynx snarled once more, then bounded up the mountainside and disappeared.

"Probably none of us will ever see such a thing again," Dad said.

Cari planted her hands on her small hips. "I hope not! Where was the deer's mother?"

"The fawn probably wandered away," Mom told her.

"Not too smart," Andy put in. "Good thing we came along and Dad has such keen eyes." He grinned. "We got to be good Samaritans, right?"

"Right," the others replied, then they climbed back in the cars and drove on.

From Colorado they headed to New Mexico. Santa Fe, the capital city, was interesting. The older part had low buildings made of adobe, dried mud. Most were the color of the earth in that part of the country: orange-red. Some were painted pale pink, yellow, blue, or green.

At last they reached Albuquerque. Many of the smiling, dark-skinned people came from families that originally lived in Mexico. Some wore brightly colored clothing. Handmade silver and turquoise Indian jewelry was for sale in all the stores.

It felt good to stay inside after so many nights camping out. Mom's sister and her family were overjoyed to see the travelers. They took them on short trips to see the sights around Albuquerque. One day they all went up into the Jemez Mountains (pronounced *Hame-us)* for a picnic.

When they started home, the Reynoldses' car wouldn't start. Uncle Ned said he'd try to tow them, but what they really needed was a tow truck.

"God sent a water truck. He can send a tow truck, too," Andy reminded them. The three families asked God to please send help.

Dad had barely finished saying "Amen" when a big heavy truck stopped alongside them. An old rancher with a wide hat and tanned, weather-wrinkled face called to them, "Is your car dead?"

"Dead or sound asleep!" Dad replied. "If you'll tow us to where we can roll the rest of the way down to a service station, we'll be glad to pay you."

The rancher grunted. "Let's just get you hitched up." They did, and the old man towed them for miles and miles down the curving road, with Uncle Ned's car following. The man shook his head when they reached the service station and Dad held out money. "I figure the good Lord put us here to help each other," he said. "Just pass the help on to someone else." He unhitched the tow chain, climbed into his truck, and drove away. The three families knew they would never forget the kind man Cari called their "New Mexico Good Samaritan."

All too soon the travelers had to say goodbye and start for home. Cari rubbed her eyes and said, "It's hard to leave."

"I know." Andy looked out the car window at the red dirt, the red water in the Colorado River, and the red adobe houses. "They liked having me play my guitar. Can, I mean, may we come again?"

"Maybe someday." Dad carefully merged onto the freeway leading west. "Cheer up, family. We have a lot more to see before we get back to Darrington, starting with another parade."

Another parade! Cari and Andy forgot all about being sad. ●

18

"Torn Hoad"

Cari Reynolds laughed when Dad said the parade was in Gallup. "Giddyap, horsey!"

"Not that kind of gallop," Mom told her. "Gallup is the trading center of many Southwest tribes of Native Americans. Every year they have a festival. We're fortunate to be here for it."

Thousands of people came for the celebration. After the travelers parked and hurried back to the long main street, they could hear the beat of drums. The parade would start any minute.

A friendly man moved aside so Andy and Cari could sit on the curb with other children. "Here they come," the man said. "Almost every western tribe sent members."

The drums beat more loudly. Then a famous

army general rode down the street on a cream-colored horse, the only White person in the long parade. Andy had seen him on TV. "It was a great honor for him to be chosen by the tribes to lead the parade," Dad whispered.

Native Americans in Indian clothing, feathers, beads, and silver and turquoise jewelry followed. They marched, danced, and let out war cries. More and more came. The friendly man said the parade was more than a mile long. No one left the sidewalk until the last colorful group passed.

"This reminds us of how different things were long ago when White people and Native Americans fought over the land," Mom said. "I'm glad those days are gone forever."

"So am I." "Me too," the children chorused.

Leaving Gallup, the travelers drove into Arizona. "Why does the ground look like a rainbow?" Cari asked. The others stared with her. Brilliant pink, blue, yellow, red, and purple covered the ground. The cars pulled off the road. Everyone got out. Cari gasped. "They're flowers. Itsy-bitsy, teeny-tiny flowers!"

"We probably won't see this again," Uncle Ned explained. "It must have rained recently. The flower seeds lie hidden in the ground for months or years. When it rains, they sprout and bloom."

Cari couldn't take her gaze off the flowers, but Uncle Ned pointed to a tall plant with spiky-looking leaves at the bottom. A cluster of greenish-white blossoms sat near the top of the stalk. "That's called a Century Plant. People used to think they only bloomed once every 100 years. Actually they bloom oftener, some every year. They grow 20 to 30 feet high in one season!"

"There's a barrel cactus." Dad waved at a spiny cactus with yellow flowers on top. "God made it special, too. Indians used to use the tough curved spines for fishhooks. It also contains juicy pulp that has saved lives of persons caught in the desert without water."

"It looks like Porky Pine," Cari said, then went back to admiring the wildflower carpet.

"Don't touch any of the cacti," Auntie Hester warned. "Many have sharp spines."

The two families climbed back in their cars. A few miles later a large bird with a long tail darted in front of them. "Roadrunner," Dad said. He braked and slowed. The strange-looking bird ran just ahead of them. Dad clocked it on the speedometer. The bird was running 15 miles an hour! He touched the gas, and the roadrunner darted off the road to safety. "Roadrunners are also called snake killers," Dad told the family. "They use their speed for protection against enemies."

The families stopped at a roadside attraction and

saw many creatures that didn't live near Darrington. Rattlesnakes coiled in circles behind heavy glass. Mom said God gave them rattles to warn their enemies to keep away. Another display held enormous hairy spiders called tarantulas. Cari looked, then ran behind her mother, but Andy read the card next to the case. "Don't be afraid. Their bite is no worse than a bee sting," he reported.

"They're too scary!" His sister examined another cage. "Is that a snake?" She stared at a fat creature with a stumpy tail and orange and brown-black markings.

"No, a Gila *(hee-luh)* monster. It's actually a lizard, and poisonous. Guess what! Mother Gila monsters bury their eggs, and the heat of the sun hatches them."

"They look like Ally Gator and Crocky Dile," Cari said. "What did God do for them?"

"We'll find out when we get back in the car," Andy promised. When they did, he turned to the pictures of an alligator and a crocodile. "They're alike, but different, like us. God gave both short, strong legs for walking. They swim by swinging their tails back and forth! Their eyes stick up so they can see above the water. Crocodiles are meaner and have pointed snouts."

That night when they camped, Andy saw something move in a pile of leaves. His sharp eyes spotted what looked like a toad with horns and spiny skin like a cactus. "Come see," he called.

Both families went to where he was. Uncle Ned laughed. "That's a horned toad, really a lizard. See how he blends into where he lives? Those spines protect him from enemies. Don't disturb him. When something does, horned toads spurt little drops of blood from their eyes."

"Does it hurt him?" Cari wanted to know.

"No, honey. It's just the way God made horned toads," Uncle Ned quickly told her. They watched the curious creature until it slipped beneath the leaves, but Cari said she liked the "torn hoad" better than anything they had seen in Arizona! ●

19

Secrets of the Canyon

How would you like to take a detour?" Dad asked his family and Uncle Ned's. "Let's swing back into Colorado and see Mesa Verde."

"May see birdie? What a funny name!" Cari giggled. "What kind of birdies?"

Dad smiled. *"May-suh-vur-dee,* honey. Spanish for 'green table.' It's covered with forests. We'll see birds and animals, but the canyon also has a secret."

Andy stopped writing in the Trip Journal and sat bolt upright. "A secret! What is it?"

Dad looked mysterious. "Cliff dwellings. Hundreds of years ago people built homes in the enormous rock walls for protection against other tribes. Some of the cliff dwellings were 2-4 stories high. Several had between 100 and 200 living rooms! It's believed that at one time 400 people lived in Cliff Palace, the largest structure."

"What's the secret?" Cari wanted to know.

"Suddenly the cliff dwellers abandoned their homes," Dad said. "Historians believe they left in the late 1200s because of a great drought, but no one knows for sure."

"I can hardly wait to get there!" Andy shouted. All the way north he wished Dad would drive faster. At last they reached the canyons with their overhanging walls and room enough for a hundred secrets. Up they climbed to the Visitors Center, where they parked and took a trail to the cliff dwellings.

"It's kind of spooky," Andy said. "Like that old deserted mining ghost town we saw."

"The underground rooms you see were kivas (kee-vuhs). The Indians held religious ceremonies there," Dad explained. "I must confess, I like our church in Darrington better." His eyes twinkled.

"Did you like Mesa Verde?" Mom asked when they started back down the mountainside.

"Yes," the children said. "It made me feel weird, though," Andy added. "Once hundreds of persons lived here. Boys my age probably helped their dads find food. Girls like Cari helped their mothers. Then pouf!" He snapped his fingers.

"They all disappeared."

"That's the secret," Cari reminded. It made her brother laugh.

"Off to the Grand Canyon," Dad sang. "It may have a secret, too."

The canyon did have a secret, but before the travelers learned it, they saw countless other interesting things at the South Rim, including red, pink, cream, and orange cliffs. The canyon was so deep they had to stare hard to see the Colorado River at the bottom. It looked like a tiny winding ribbon. Native Americans performed for the tourists. Roadside stands and little shops offered polished rocks, jewelry, and brightly colored handmade bowls and blankets.

Cari loved the many tiny striped chipmunks that ran with their tails up in the air and didn't seem afraid of people. "What did God do for them?" she asked. "Besides help them run fast?"

"He taught them to dig," Andy answered. He'd been reading his animal books and felt proud to report what he'd learned. "They make tunnels in the ground, push the dirt out, and build their nests underground where it's safe. And they store food there, too. On warm winter days, chipmunks sometimes wake up from their winter naps and eat part of their food."

"If we're going to reach the North Rim tonight, we'd best be going," Mom reminded.

Miles and miles of forest and meadow stretched between the turnoff at Jacob Lake and the North Rim. The travelers saw their first wild turkeys, plus many deer and other animals. After they reached the campground and set up, Andy saw a notice about a park ranger talk that night. His heart pounded. "Maybe the ranger will tell us the secret of the canyon," he exclaimed.

The well-informed ranger showed gorgeous slides of the canyon. Then he said, real mysterious-like, "The North Rim of the Canyon where we are sitting is between 8,000 and 9,000 feet above sea level. Yet people have found *clam shells* here."

Clam shells! How did clams get hundreds of miles away from the ocean and thousands of feet up in the air? Andy burned to ask Mom and Dad about it.

"No one can say for sure," Dad quietly said as they went back to camp. "Mom and I believe it may have happened in the time of Noah. The Bible says after Noah obeyed God and built the ark, waters covered the earth." Dad smiled. "It's the only way I know to solve the mystery."

"Sounds good to me." Andy yawned. So did Cari. After a quick prayer, they hopped into bed, still thinking of the secrets of the canyons and wondering what they'd see the next day. ●

Andy should have known they
wouldn't forget his birthday.

20

Surprises and Secrets

The travelers left the canyon country and started home. Nevada wasn't too interesting, so the children turned to their books. One listed unusual animals. Andy read them out loud. "Hey, aardvark *(ahrd vahrk)* means 'earth pig' because of its long snout. It lives in Africa and catches insects with its 18-inch sticky tongue! I'll bet our *World Book* at home has a picture of it."

"Tell me some other animals," Cari begged.

"There are giant anteaters in Central and South America."

The girl looked worried. "They won't eat Auntie Hester, will they?"

Andy laughed. "Anteaters don't eat people! They're like aardvarks and scoop up ants with their tongues. Some anteaters live in trees. They wrap their long tails around the branches so they won't fall." Later he turned to a picture of a mother opossum carrying four babies on her back. "Opossums hang by their tails, too."

"Leave your books for another day," Mom told the children. "It's getting too dark to read."

They didn't see any towns or campsites for many miles. Everyone was so tired by the time they found a motel that they grabbed their pajamas and toothbrushes and left everything else in the car.

A sound awakened Andy early the next morning. Had their car started? *No way,* he thought, and went back to sleep. A few hours later, he wished he hadn't. Dad stepped outside and discovered their car was gone! Fear squeezed Andy's stomach. How would they get home?

"We need to pray hard," Dad said. "Our clothes are gone and we don't have money to stay here long." The families knelt down and asked God for help.

Andy and Cari sat in the motel room or walked around the parking lot. They wished they had their books to read, but they were in the car. Mom looked worried. Dad paced the floor. Andy kept praying that they would get their car back.

Hours later police officers brought it to the motel, dusty but unharmed. "You're lucky," they told Mom and Dad. "Thieves often strip cars."

"Not lucky," Dad told them. "We asked God to help us and He did." When the police had gone, the two families knelt in prayer to thank God for returning their car.

A few days later the travelers reached Oregon. Soon they would turn down the Columbia River Gorge toward Portland to see Uncle Al and Aunt Ruth. Uncle Ned went on ahead. When the others reached the agreed-on meeting point, his Plymouth wasn't there. The Reynoldses waited and waited. Then, "Hey, there they go!" Andy shouted when Uncle Ned's car roared past.

"Stop, Uncle Ned!" Cari called, but no one in the other car heard.

"They must have stopped for gas or thought we were to meet on the other side of town." Dad chuckled. "We travel thousands of miles together and only get separated this close to home!"

"We're chasing Uncle Ned and he thinks he's chasing us!" Andy howled with laughter. "I have to write this in our Trip Journal." *And that it's my birthday,* he silently added with a sigh. *Mom and Dad must have forgotten because of losing the car.* Then he thought, *Don't be stupid. An 11-year-old boy should be old enough not to care if he didn't have a celebration and one of Mom's special cakes.* Yet Andy did.

They caught up with Uncle Ned at their relatives' driveway. Everyone laughed as they told each other what had happened. They laughed even harder when Auntie Ruth brought out an enormous cake. "Surprise! Happy birthday, Andy!"

Andy felt himself get red. He should have known Mom and Dad wouldn't forget his birthday.

The travelers arrived home the next day. Each knelt and thanked God for all the things He had done for them. They thanked Him for the gift of His Son. And for the many exciting secrets they would one day learn after Jesus came to take them home to heaven. Cari sang a new song.

"God did neat things for the kangaroo,
  And for the other animals, too.
  But He sent Jesus for me and you."

That night Andy stared out his window at the Darrington stars. "I learned another secret today, God. It's fun going places, but coming home is even better." He grinned. "It's going to be some trip when You take us home to heaven!" He yawned and dropped back on his pillow. "Mom always says every end is a new beginning. I can hardly wait to find out what's next."

★ ★ ★

In *Secrets of the Sea* Andy, Cari, and their parents discover a whole new world of "curious critters" and learn all the wonderful things God did for them.